ABRIDGED CLASSICS

THREE MEN IN A BOAT

(To say nothing of the dog).

Written by
Jerome K. Jerome

Abridged by
Sonal Talwar

Illustrated by
Tanoy Choudhury

Contents

Pre-Reading Activities 3
1. Chapter I 4
2. Chapter II 14
3. Chapter III 21
4. Chapter IV 29
5. Chapter V 38
6. Chapter VI 49
7. Chapter VII 56
8. Chapter VIII 65
9. Chapter IX 70
10. Chapter X 71
11. Chapter XI 75
12. Chapter XII 81
13. Chapter XIII 85
14. Chapter XIV 93
15. Chapter XV 96
16. Chapter XVI 104
17. Chapter XVII 113
18. Chapter XVIII 124
Post-Reading Activities 144

Pre-Reading Activities

Discuss

1. Have you ever been on a boat trip? Discuss your experience.

Writing

2. What do you know about the Hampton Court Maze?

3. What does the title suggest to you?

4. Write about River Thames.

5. Where would you like to go on a holiday with your friends?

Chapter I

There were four of us—George, and William Samuel Harris, and myself, and Montmorency. We were sitting in my room, smoking, and talking about how bad we were—bad from a medical point of view I mean, of course.

We were all feeling seedy, and we were getting quite nervous about it. Harris said he felt such extraordinary fits of giddiness come over him at times, that he hardly knew what he was doing. And then George said that *he* had fits of giddiness too, and hardly knew what *he* was doing. With me, it was my liver that was out of order. I remember going to the British Museum one day to read up the treatment for some slight ailment of which I had a touch—hay fever, I fancy it was. I got down the book, and read all I came to read; and then, in an unthinking moment, I idly turned the leaves, and began to indolently study diseases, generally. I sat for awhile, frozen with horror; and then, in the listlessness of despair, I again turned over the pages. I came to typhoid fever—read the symptoms—discovered that I had typhoid fever, must have had it for months without knowing it—wondered what else I had got; turned up St. Vitus's Dance—

J in the British Museum

found, as I expected, that I had that too,—began to get interested in my case, and determined to sift it to the bottom, and so started alphabetically—read up ague, and learnt that I was sickening for it, and that the acute stage would commence in about another fortnight. Cholera I had, with severe complications; and diphtheria I seemed to have been born with. I plodded conscientiously through the twenty-six letters, and the only malady I could conclude I had not got was housemaid's knee.

I sat and pondered. I thought what an interesting case I must be from a medical point of view, what an acquisition I should be to a class! Students would have no need to "walk the hospitals," if they had me. I was a hospital in myself. All they need do would be to walk round me, and, after that, take their diploma.

Then I wondered how long I had to live. I had walked into that reading-room a happy, healthy man. I crawled out a decrepit wreck.

I went to my medical man. He is an old chum of mine, and feels my pulse, and looks at my tongue, and talks about the weather, all for nothing, when I fancy I'm ill. So I thought I would do him a good turn by going to him now. "What a doctor wants," I said, "is practice. He shall have me. He will get more practice out of me than out of seventeen hundred of your ordinary, commonplace patients, with only one or two diseases each." So I went straight up and saw him, and he said:

"Well, what's the matter with you?"

I said:

"I will not take up your time, dear boy, with telling you what is the matter with me. Life is brief, and you might pass away before I had finished. But I will tell you what is *not* the matter with me. I have not got housemaid's knee. Everything else, however, I *have* got."

Then he opened me and looked down me, and clutched hold of my wrist, and then he hit me over the chest when I wasn't expecting it—a cowardly thing to do, I call it—and immediately afterwards butted me with the side of his head. After that, he sat down and wrote out a prescription, and folded it up and gave it me, and I put it in my pocket and went out.

I did not open it. I took it to the nearest chemist's, and handed it in. The man read it, and then handed it back.

He said he didn't keep it.

I read the prescription. It ran:

"1 lb. beefsteak, with 1 pt. bitter beer every 6 hours.

J with the doctor

1 ten-mile walk every morning.

1 bed at 11 sharp every night.

And don't stuff up your head with things you don't understand."

I followed the directions, with the happy result—speaking for myself—that my life was preserved, and is still going on.

You know, it often is so—those simple, old-fashioned remedies are sometimes more efficacious than all the dispensary stuff.

We sat there for half-an-hour, describing to each other our maladies. I explained to George and William Harris how I felt when I got up in the morning, and William Harris told us how he felt when he went to bed; and George stood on the hearth-rug, and gave us a clever and powerful piece of acting, illustrative of how he felt in the night.

George *fancies* he is ill; but there's never anything really the matter with him, you know.

What it was that was actually the matter with us, we none of us could be sure of; but the unanimous opinion was that it—whatever it was—had been brought on by overwork.

"What we want is rest," said Harris.

"Rest and a complete change," said George.

I agreed with George, and suggested that we should seek out some retired and old-world spot, far from the madding crowd, and dream away a sunny week among its drowsy lanes—some half-forgotten nook, hidden away by the fairies, out of reach of the noisy world—some quaint-perched eyrie on the cliffs of Time, from whence the surging waves of the nineteenth century would sound far-off and faint.

Harris said he thought it would be humpy. He said he knew the sort of place I meant; where everybody went to bed at eight o'clock, and you couldn't get a *Referee* for love or money, and had to walk ten miles to get your baccy.

"No," said Harris, "if you want rest and change, you can't beat a sea trip."

I objected to the sea trip strongly. A sea trip does you good when you are going to have a couple of months of it, but, for a week, it is wicked.

George said he should be all right, and would rather like it, but he would advise Harris and me not to think of it, as he felt sure we should both be ill. Harris said that, to himself, it was always a mystery how people managed to get sick at sea—said he thought people must do it on purpose, from affectation—said he had often wished to be, but had never been able.

It is a curious fact, but nobody ever is sea-sick — on land. At sea, you come across plenty of people very bad indeed, whole boat-loads of them; but I never met a man yet, on land, who had ever known at all what it was to be sea-sick. Where the thousands upon thousands of bad sailors that swarm in every ship hide themselves when they are on land is a mystery.

For myself, I have discovered an excellent preventive against sea-sickness, in balancing myself. You stand in the centre of the deck, and, as the ship heaves and pitches, you move your body about, so as to keep it always straight. When the front of the ship rises, you lean forward, till the deck almost touches your nose; and when its back end gets up, you lean backwards. This is all very well for an hour or two; but you can't balance yourself for a week.

George said:

"Let's go up the river."

He said we should have fresh air, exercise and quiet; the constant change of scene would occupy our minds and the hard work would give us a good appetite, and make us sleep well.

Harris said he didn't think George ought to do anything that would have a tendency to make him sleepier than he always was, as it might be

George, Harris, J and Montmorency

dangerous. He said he didn't very well understand how George was going to sleep any more than he did now, seeing that there were only twenty-four hours in each day, summer and winter alike; but thought that if he *did* sleep any more, he might just as well be dead, and so save his board and lodging.

Harris said, however, that the river would suit him to a "T." I don't know what a "T" is (except a sixpenny one, which includes bread-and-butter and cake *ad lib.*, and is cheap at the price, if you haven't had any dinner). It seems to suit everybody, however, which is greatly to its credit.

It suited me to a "T" too, and Harris and I both said it was a good idea of George's; and we said it in a tone that seemed to somehow imply that we were surprised that George should have come out so sensible.

The only one who was not struck with the suggestion was Montmorency. He never did care for the river, did Montmorency.

We were three to one, however, and the motion was carried.

Chapter II

We pulled out the maps, and discussed plans. We arranged to start on the following Saturday from Kingston. Harris and I would go down in the morning, and take the boat up to Chertsey, and George, who would not be able to get away from the City till the afternoon would meet us there.

Should we "camp out" or sleep at inns?

George and I were for camping out. We said it would be so wild and free, so patriarchal like.

Slowly the golden memory of the dead sun fades from the hearts of the cold, sad clouds. Silent, like sorrowing children, the birds have ceased their song, and only the moorhen's plaintive cry and the harsh croak of the corncrake stirs the awed hush around the couch of waters, where the dying day breathes out her last.

From the dim woods on either bank, Night's ghostly army, the grey shadows, creep out with noiseless tread to chase away the lingering rear-guard of the light, and pass, with noiseless, unseen feet, above the waving river-grass, and through the sighing rushes. And Night, upon her sombre throne, folds her black wings above the darkening world, and, from her phantom palace, lit by the pale stars, reigns in stillness.

Then we run our little boat into some quiet nook, and the tent is pitched, and the frugal supper cooked and eaten. Then the big pipes are filled and lighted, and the pleasant chat goes round in musical undertone; while, in the pauses of our talk, the river, playing round the boat, prattles strange old tales and secrets, sings low the old child's song that it has sung so many thousand years—will sing so many thousand years to come, before its voice grows harsh and old—a song that we, who have learnt to love its changing face, who have so often nestled on its yielding bosom, think, somehow, we understand, though we could not tell you in mere words the story that we listen to.

And we sit there, by its margin, while the moon, who loves it too, stoops down to kiss it with a sister's kiss, and throws her silver arms around it clingingly.

Harris said:

"How about when it rained?"

You can never rouse Harris. There is no poetry about Harris—no wild yearning for the unattainable. Harris never "weeps, he knows not why." If Harris's eyes fill with tears, you can bet

Beautiful nature

it is because Harris has been eating raw onions, or has put too much Worcester over his chop.

If you were to stand at night by the sea-shore with Harris, and say:

"Hark! do you not hear? Is it but the mermaids singing deep below the waving waters; or sad spirits, chanting dirges for white corpses, held by seaweed?" Harris would take you by the arm, and say:

"I know what it is, old man; you've got a chill. Now, you come along with me. I know a place round the corner here, where you can get a drop of the finest Scotch whisky you ever tasted—put you right in less than no time."

Harris always does know a place round the corner where you can get something brilliant in the drinking line. I believe that if you met Harris up in Paradise (supposing such a thing likely), he would immediately greet you with:

"So glad you've come, old fellow; I've found a nice place round the corner here, where you can get some really first-class nectar."

In the present instance, however, as regarded the camping out, his practical view of the matter came as a very timely hint. Camping out in rainy weather is not pleasant.

We therefore decided that we would sleep out on fine nights; and hotel it, and inn it, and pub. it, like respectable folks, when it was wet, or when we felt inclined for a change.

Montmorency hailed this compromise with much approval. He does not revel in romantic solitude. Give him something noisy; and if a trifle low, so much the jollier. To look at Montmorency you would imagine that he was an angel sent upon the earth, for some reason withheld from mankind, in the shape of a small fox-terrier. There is a sort of Oh-what-a-wicked-world-this-is-and-how-I-wish-I-could-do-something-to-make-it-better-and-nobler expression about Montmorency that has been known to bring the tears into the eyes of pious old ladies and gentlemen.

When first he came to live at my expense, I never thought I should be able to get him to stop long. I used to sit down and look at him, as he sat on the rug and looked up at me, and think: "Oh, that dog will never live. He will be snatched up to the bright skies in a chariot that is what will happen to him."

But, when I paid for about a dozen chickens that he killed; and dragged him, growling and kicking, by the scruff of his neck, out of a hundred and fourteen street fights; and had had a dead cat brought round for my inspection by an irritated

George and J. in conversation

female, had won thirty shillings by backing him to kill rats against time, then I began to think that maybe they'd let him remain on earth for a bit longer, after all.

To hang about a stable, and collect a gang of the most disreputable dogs to be found in the town, and lead them out to march round the slums to fight other disreputable dogs, is Montmorency's idea of "life;" and so, as I before observed, he gave to the suggestion of inns, and pubs., and hotels his most emphatic approbation.

Having thus settled the sleeping arrangements to the satisfaction of all four of us, the only thing left to discuss was what we should take with us; and this we had begun to argue, when Harris said he'd had enough oratory for one night, and proposed that we should go out and have a smile, saying that he had found a place, round by the square, where you could really get a drop of Irish worth drinking.

George said he felt thirsty and, as I had a presentiment that a little whisky, warm, with a slice of lemon, would do my complaint good, the debate was, by common assent, adjourned to the following night; and the assembly put on its hats and went out.

Chapter III

So, on the following evening, we again assembled, to discuss and arrange our plans. Harris said:

"Now, the first thing to settle is what to take with us. Now, you get a bit of paper and write down, J., and you get the grocery catalogue, George, and somebody give me a bit of pencil, and then I'll make out a list."

That's Harris all over—so ready to take the burden of everything himself, and put it on the backs of other people.

He always reminds me of my poor Uncle Podger. You never saw such a commotion up and down a house, in all your life, as when my Uncle Podger undertook to do a job. A picture would have come home from the frame-maker's, and be standing in the dining-room, waiting to be put up; and Aunt Podger would ask what was to be done with it, and Uncle Podger would say:

"Oh, you leave that to *me*. Don't you, any of you, worry yourselves about that. *I'll* do all that."

I remember how Uncle Podger once caused disorder for his entire household when he was

George, Harris and J making a list of things

trying to complete the simple job of hammering a nail into the wall.

Harris will be just that sort of man when he grows up, I know, and I told him so. I said I could not permit him to take so much labour upon himself. I said:

"No; *you* get the paper, and the pencil, and the catalogue, and George write down, and I'll do the work."

The first list we made out had to be discarded. It was clear that the upper reaches of the Thames would not allow of the navigation of a boat sufficiently large to take the things we had set down as indispensable; so we tore the list up, and looked at one another!

George said:

"You know we are on a wrong track altogether. We must not think of the things we could do with, but only of the things that we can't do without."

George comes out really quite sensible at times. You'd be surprised. I call that downright wisdom, not merely as regards the present case, but with reference to our trip up the river of life, generally. How many people, on that voyage, load up the boat till it is ever in danger of swamping with a store of foolish things which they think essential to the pleasure and comfort of the trip, but which are really only useless lumber.

Well, we left the list to George, and he began it.

"We won't take a tent," suggested George; "we will have a boat with a cover. It is ever so much simpler, and more comfortable."

It seemed a good thought, and we adopted it. I do not know whether you have ever seen the thing I mean. You fix iron hoops up over the boat, and stretch a huge canvas over them, and fasten it down all round, from stem to stern, and it converts the boat into a sort of little house, and it is beautifully cosy, though a trifle stuffy; but there, everything has its drawbacks, as the man said when his mother-in-law died, and they came down upon him for the funeral expenses.

George said that in that case we must take a rug each, a lamp, some soap, a brush and comb (between us), a toothbrush (each), a basin, some tooth-powder, some shaving tackle (sounds like a French exercise, doesn't it?), and a couple of big-towels for bathing. I notice that people always make gigantic arrangements for bathing when they are going anywhere near the water, but that they don't bathe much when they are there.

It is the same when you go to the sea-side. I always determine—when thinking over the matter in London—that I'll get up early every morning, and go and have a dip before breakfast, and I religiously pack up a pair of drawers and a bath towel. I always get red bathing drawers. I rather fancy myself in red drawers. But when I get to the sea I don't feel somehow that I want that early morning bathe nearly so much as I did when I was in town.

On the contrary, I feel more that I want to stop in bed till the last moment, and then come down and have my breakfast. Once or twice virtue has triumphed, and I have got out at six and half-dressed myself, and have taken my drawers and towel, and stumbled dismally off. But I haven't enjoyed it. They seem to keep a specially cutting east wind, waiting for me, when I go to bathe in the early morning. And when I do get to the sea, it is rough and quite insulting.

One huge wave catches me up and chucks me in a sitting posture, as hard as ever it can, down on to a rock which has been put there for me. And, before I've said "Oh! Ugh!" and found out what has gone, the wave comes back and carries me out to mid-ocean. I begin to strike out frantically for the shore, and wonder if I shall ever see home and friends again, and wish I'd been kinder to my little sister when a boy (when I was a boy, I mean). Just when I have given up all hope, a wave retires and

Boat with the cover

leaves me sprawling like a star-fish on the sand, and I get up and look back and find that I've been swimming for my life in two feet of water. I hop back and dress, and crawl home, where I have to pretend I liked it.

In the present instance, we all talked as if we were going to have a long swim every morning.

George said it was so pleasant to wake up in the boat in the fresh morning, and plunge into the limpid river. Harris said there was nothing like a swim before breakfast to give you an appetite. He said it always gave him an appetite. George said that if it was going to make Harris eat more than Harris ordinarily ate, then he should protest against Harris having a bath at all.

He said there would be quite enough hard work in towing sufficient food for Harris up against stream, as it was.

I urged upon George, however, how much pleasanter it would be to have Harris clean and fresh about the boat, even if we did have to take a few more hundredweight of provisions; and he got to see it in my light, and withdrew his opposition to Harris's bath.

Agreed, finally, that we should take *three* bath towels, so as not to keep each other waiting.

For clothes, George said two suits of flannel would be sufficient, as we could wash them ourselves, in the river, when they got dirty. We asked him if he had ever tried washing flannels in the river, and he replied: "No, not exactly himself like; but he knew some fellows who had, and it was easy enough;" and Harris and I were weak enough to fancy he knew what he was talking about, and that three respectable young men, without position or influence, and with no experience in washing, could really clean their own shirts and trousers in the river Thames with a bit of soap.

George impressed upon us to take a change of under-things and plenty of socks, in case we got upset and wanted a change; also plenty of handkerchiefs, as they would do to wipe things, and a pair of leather boots as well as our boating shoes, as we should want them if we got upset.

Chapter IV

Then we discussed the food question. George said:

"Begin with breakfast." (George is so practical.) "Now for breakfast we shall want a frying-pan" — (Harris said it was indigestible; but we merely urged him not to be an ass, and George went on) — "a tea-pot and a kettle, and a methylated spirit stove."

"No oil," said George, with a significant look; and Harris and I agreed.

We had taken up an oil-stove once, but "never again." It had been like living in an oil-shop that week. It oozed. I never saw such a thing as paraffine oil is to ooze. We kept it in the nose of the boat, and, from there, it oozed down to the rudder, impregnating the whole boat and everything in it on its way, and it oozed over the river, and saturated the scenery and spoilt the atmosphere.

Therefore, in the present instance, we confined ourselves to methylated spirit.

For other breakfast things, George suggested eggs and bacon, which were easy to cook, cold meat, tea, bread and butter, and jam. For lunch, he said, we could have biscuits, cold meat, bread

Everything piled up in aheap on the floor

and butter, and jam—but *no cheese*. Cheese, like oil, makes too much of itself. It wants the whole boat to itself. It goes through the hamper, and gives a cheesy flavour to everything else there. You can't tell whether you are eating apple-pie or German sausage, or strawberries and cream. It all seems cheese. There is too much odour about cheese.

"We shan't want any tea," said George (Harris's face fell at this); "but we'll have a good round, square, slap-up meal at seven—dinner, tea, and supper combined."

Harris grew more cheerful. George suggested meat and fruit pies, cold meat, tomatoes, fruit, and green stuff. For drink, we took some wonderful sticky concoction of Harris's, which you mixed with water and called lemonade, plenty of tea, and a bottle of whisky, in case, as George said, we got upset.

It seemed to me that George harped too much on the getting-upset idea. It seemed to me the wrong spirit to go about the trip in.

But I'm glad we took the whisky.

We didn't take beer or wine. They are a mistake up the river. They make you feel sleepy and heavy. A glass in the evening when you are doing a mouch round the town and looking at the girls is all right enough; but don't drink when the sun is blazing down on your head, and you've got hard work to do.

We made a list of the things to be taken, and a pretty lengthy one it was, before we parted that evening. The next day, which was Friday, we got them all together, and met in the evening to pack. We got a big Gladstone for the clothes, and a couple of hampers for the victuals and the cooking utensils. We moved the table up against the window, piled everything in a heap in the middle of the floor, and sat round and looked at it.

I said I'd pack.

I rather pride myself on my packing. George put on a pipe and spread himself over the easy-chair, and Harris cocked his legs on the table and lit a cigar.

This was hardly what I intended. What I had meant, of course, was, that I should boss the job, and that Harris and George should potter about under my directions.

However, I did not say anything, but started the packing. It seemed a longer job than I had thought it was going to be; but I got the bag finished at last, and I sat on it and strapped it.

"Ain't you going to put the boots in?" said Harris.

And I looked round, and found I had forgotten them. That's just like Harris. He couldn't have said a word until I'd got the bag shut and strapped, of course. And George laughed — one of those irritating, senseless, chuckle-headed, crack-jawed laughs of his. They do make me so wild.

I opened the bag and packed the boots in; and then, just as I was going to close it, a horrible idea occurred to me. Had I packed my tooth-brush? I don't know how it is, but I never do know whether I've packed my tooth-brush.

My tooth-brush is a thing that haunts me when I'm travelling, and makes my life a misery. I dream that I haven't packed it, and wake up in a cold perspiration, and get out of bed and hunt for it.

And, in the morning, I pack it before I have used it, and have to unpack again to get it, and it is always the last thing I turn out of the bag; and then I repack and forget it, and have to rush upstairs for it at the last moment and carry it to the railway station, wrapped up in my pocket-handkerchief.

Of course I had to turn every mortal thing out now, and, of course, I could not find it. I rummaged the things up into much the same state that they must have been before the world was created, and when chaos reigned.

Harris packing strawberry jam over tomato

Of course, I found George's and Harris's eighteen times over, but I couldn't find my own. I put the things back one by one, and held everything up and shook it. Then I found it inside a boot. I repacked once more.

When I had finished, George asked if the soap was in. I said I didn't care a hang whether the soap was in or whether it wasn't; and I slammed the bag to and strapped it, and found that I had packed my tobacco-pouch in it, and had to re-open it.

It got shut up finally at 10.5 p.m., and then there remained the hampers to do. Harris said that we should be wanting to start in less than twelve hours' time, and thought that he and George had better do the rest; and I agreed and sat down, and they had a go.

They began in a light-hearted spirit, evidently intending to show me how to do it. I made no comment; I only waited.

It did. They started with breaking a cup. That was the first thing they did. They did that just to show you what they *could* do, and to get you interested.

Then Harris packed the strawberry jam on top of a tomato and squashed it, and they had to pick out the tomato with a teaspoon.

And then it was George's turn, and he trod on the butter. They upset salt over everything, and as for the butter! I never saw two men do more with one-and-two pence worth of butter in my whole life than they did.

After George had got it off his slipper, they tried to put it in the kettle. It wouldn't go in, and what *was* in wouldn't come out.

They did scrape it out at last, and put it down on a chair, and Harris sat on it, and it stuck to him, and they went looking for it all over the room.

Then George got round at the back of Harris and saw it.

And they got it off, and packed it in the teapot.

Montmorency was in it all, of course. Montmorency's ambition in life, is to get in the way and be sworn at.

If he can squirm in anywhere where he particularly is not wanted, and be a perfect nuisance, and make people mad, and have things thrown at his head, then he feels his day has not been wasted.

To get somebody to stumble over him, and curse him steadily for an hour, is his highest aim and object; and, when he has succeeded in accomplishing this, his conceit becomes quite unbearable.

He came and sat down on things, just when they were wanted to be packed; and he laboured under the fixed belief that, whenever Harris or George reached out their hand for anything, it was his cold, damp nose that they wanted.

The packing was done at 12.50. We were all ready for bed. Harris was to sleep with us that night, and we went upstairs.

George said:

"What time shall I wake you fellows?"

"Wake us at 6.30, George," we said.

Chapter V

It was Mrs. Poppets that woke me up next morning.

She said:

"Do you know that it's nearly nine o'clock, sir?"

"Nine o' what?" I cried, starting up.

"Nine o'clock," she replied, through the keyhole. "I thought you was a-oversleeping yourselves."

I woke Harris, and told him. He said:

"I thought you wanted to get up at six?"

"So I did," I answered; "why didn't you wake me?"

"How could I wake you, when you didn't wake me?" he retorted. "Now we shan't get on the water till after twelve. I wonder you take the trouble to get up at all."

"Um," I replied, "lucky for you that I do. If I hadn't woke you, you'd have lain there for the whole fortnight."

We snarled at one another in this strain for the next few minutes, when we were interrupted by a defiant snore from George.

Mrs. Poppets wakes up J

It reminded us, for the first time since our being called, of his existence. There he lay—the man who had wanted to know what time he should wake us—on his back, with his mouth wide open, and his knees stuck up.

We flew across and slung the clothes off him, and Harris landed him one with a slipper, and I shouted in his ear, and he awoke.

"Wasermarrer?" he observed, sitting up.

"Get up, you fat-headed chunk!" roared Harris. "It's quarter to ten."

"What!" he shrieked, jumping out of bed into the bath; "Who the thunder put this thing here?"

We told him he must have been a fool not to see the bath.

We finished dressing, and, when it came to the extras, we remembered that we had packed the tooth-brushes and the brush and comb, and we had to go downstairs, and fish them out of the bag. We went downstairs to breakfast.

Montmorency had invited two other dogs to come and see him off, and they were whiling away the time by fighting on the doorstep.

We calmed them with an umbrella, and sat down to chops and cold beef.

George got hold of the paper, and read us out the boating fatalities, and the weather forecast, which latter prophesied "rain, cold, wet to fine occasional local thunder-storms, east wind, with general depression over the Midland Counties (London and Channel). Bar falling."

I do think that, of all the silly, irritating tomfoolishness by which we are plagued, this "weather-forecast" fraud is about the most aggravating.

It "forecasts" precisely what happened yesterday or the day before, and precisely the opposite of what is going to happen to-day.

I remember a holiday of mine being completely ruined one late autumn by our paying attention to the weather report of the local newspaper.

"Heavy showers, with thunderstorms, may be expected to-day," it would say on Monday, and so we would give up our picnic, and stop indoors all day, waiting for the rain.

And people would pass the house, going off in wagonettes and coaches as jolly and merry as could be, the sun shining out, and not a cloud to be seen.

"Ah!" we said, as we stood looking out at them through the window, "won't they come home soaked!"

People pass the house in wagonettes and coaches, jolly and merry

And we smiled to think how wet they were going to get, and came back and stirred the fire, and got our books, and arranged our specimens of seaweed and cockle shells.

By twelve o'clock, with the sun pouring into the room, the heat became quite oppressive, and we wondered when those heavy showers and occasional thunderstorms were going to begin.

"Ah! they'll come in the afternoon, you'll find," we said to each other. "Oh, *won't* those people get wet. What a lark!"

At one o'clock, the landlady would come in to ask if we weren't going out, as it seemed such a lovely day.

"No, no," we replied, with a knowing chuckle, "not we. *We* don't mean to get wet—no, no."

And when the afternoon was nearly gone, and still there was no sign of rain, we tried to cheer ourselves up with the idea that it would come down all at once.

It would pour just as the people started for home, and were out of the reach of any shelter, and that they would thus get more drenched than ever. But not a drop ever fell, and it finished a grand day, and a lovely night after it.

The next morning we would read that it was going to be a "warm, fine to set-fair day; much heat;" and we would dress ourselves in flimsy things, and go out.

Half-an-hour after we started, it would commence to rain hard, and a bitterly cold wind would spring up, and both would keep on steadily for the whole day.

And we would come home with colds and rheumatism all over us, and go to bed.

The weather is a thing that is beyond me altogether. I never can understand it. The barometer is useless: it is as misleading as the newspaper forecast.

It was too bright and sunny on this especial morning for George's blood-curdling readings about "Bar. falling," "atmospheric disturbance, passing in an oblique line over Southern Europe," and "pressure increasing," to very much upset us: and so, finding that he could not make us wretched, and was only wasting his time, he sneaked the cigarette that I had carefully rolled up for myself, and went.

Then Harris and I, having finished up the few things left on the table, carted out our luggage on to the doorstep, and waited for a cab.

There seemed a good deal of luggage, when we put it all together. It did look a lot, and Harris and I began to feel rather ashamed of it, though why we should be, I can't see. No cab came by, but the street boys did, and got interested in the show, apparently, and stopped.

By this time, quite a small crowd had collected, and people were asking each other what was the matter.

One party held that it was a wedding, and pointed out Harris as the bridegroom; while the elder and more thoughtful among the populace inclined to the idea that it was a funeral, and that I was probably the corpse's brother.

At last, an empty cab turned up and packing ourselves and our belongings into it, and shooting out a couple of Montmorency's friends, who had evidently sworn never to forsake him, we drove away amidst the cheers of the crowd.

We got to Waterloo at eleven, and asked where the eleven-five started from.

Of course nobody knew; nobody at Waterloo ever does know where a train is going to start from, or where a train when it does start is going to, or anything about it.

The porter who took our things thought it would go from number two platform, while another porter, with whom he discussed the question, had heard a rumour that it would go from number

On platform talking to the engine driver

one. The station-master, on the other hand, was convinced it would start from the local.

To put an end to the matter, we went upstairs, and asked the traffic superintendent, and he told us that he had just met a man, who said he had seen it at number three platform.

We went to number three platform, but the authorities there said that they rather thought that train was the Southampton express, or else the Windsor loop.

But they were sure it wasn't the Kingston train, though why they were sure it wasn't they couldn't say.

Then our porter said he thought that must be it on the high-level platform; said he thought he knew the train. So we went to the high-level platform, and saw the engine-driver, and asked him if he was going to Kingston.

He said he couldn't say for certain of course, but that he rather thought he was. Anyhow, if he wasn't the 11.5 for Kingston, he said he was pretty confident he was the 9.32 for Virginia Water, or the 10 a.m. express for the Isle of Wight, or somewhere in that direction, and we should all know when we got there.

We slipped half-a-crown into his hand, and begged him to be the 11.5 for Kingston.

Thus we got to Kingston by the London and South-Western Railway.

We learnt, afterwards, that the train we had come by was really the Exeter mail, and that they had spent hours at Waterloo, looking for it, and nobody knew what had become of it.

Our boat was waiting for us at Kingston just below bridge, and to it we wended our way, and round it we stored our luggage, and into it we stepped.

"Are you all right, sir?" said the man.

"Right it is," we answered; and with Harris at the sculls and I at the tiller-lines, and Montmorency, unhappy and deeply suspicious, in the prow, out we shot on to the waters which, for a fortnight, were to be our home.

Chapter VI

It was a glorious morning, late spring or early summer, as you care to take it, when the dainty sheen of grass and leaf is blushing to a deeper green; and the year seems like a fair young maid, trembling with strange, wakening pulses on the brink of womanhood.

The quaint back streets of Kingston, where they came down to the water's edge, looked quite picturesque in the flashing sunlight, the glinting river with its drifting barges, the wooded towpath, the trim-kept villas on the other side. Harris, in a red and orange blazer, grunting away at the sculls, the distant glimpses of the grey old palace of the Tudors, all made a sunny picture, so bright but calm, so full of life, and yet so peaceful, that, early in the day though it was, I felt myself being dreamily lulled off into a musing fit.

I mused on Kingston, or "Kyningestun," as it was once called in the days when Saxon "kinges" were crowned there. Great Cæsar crossed the river there, and the Roman legions camped upon its sloping uplands. Cæsar, like, in later years, Elizabeth, seems to have stopped everywhere: only he was more respectable than good Queen Bess; he didn't put up at the public-houses.

The quaint back streets of Kingston

Many of the old houses, round about, speak very plainly of those days when Kingston was a royal borough, and nobles and courtiers lived there, near their King, and the long road to the palace gates was gay all day with clanking steel and prancing palfreys, and rustling silks and velvets, and fair faces.

Speaking of oak staircases reminds me that there is a magnificent carved oak staircase in one of the houses in Kingston. It is a shop now, in the market-place, but it was evidently once the mansion of some great personage.

At this point Harris threw away the sculls, got up and left his seat, and sat on his back, and stuck his legs in the air. Montmorency howled, and turned a somersault, and the top hamper jumped up, and all the things came out.

I was somewhat surprised, but I did not lose my temper. I said, pleasantly enough:

"Hulloa! what's that for?"

"What's that for? Why—"

No, on second thoughts, I will not repeat what Harris said. I may have been to blame, I admit it; but nothing excuses violence of language and coarseness of expression, especially in a man who has been carefully brought up, as I know Harris has been Harris, however, said he had done enough for a bit, and proposed that I should take a turn; so, as we were in, I got out and took the tow-line, and ran the boat on past Hampton Court.

Harris asked me if I'd ever been in the maze at Hampton Court. He said he went in once to show somebody else the way. He had studied it up in a map, and it was so simple that it seemed foolish—hardly worth the two pence charged for admission. Harris said he thought that map must have been got up as a practical joke, because it wasn't a bit like the real thing, and only misleading. It was a country cousin that Harris took in. He said:

"We'll just go in here, so that you can say you've been, but it's very simple. It's absurd to call it a maze. You keep on taking the first turning to the right. We'll just walk round for ten minutes, and then go and get some lunch."

They met some people soon after they had got inside, who said they had been there for three-quarters of an hour, and had had about enough of it. Harris told them they could follow him, if they liked; he was just going in, and then should turn round and come out again. They said it was very kind of him, and fell behind, and followed.

They picked up various other people who wanted to get it over, as they went along, until they had absorbed all the persons in the maze. People who had given up all hopes of ever getting either in or out, or of ever seeing their home and friends again, plucked up courage at the sight of Harris and his party, and joined the procession, blessing him. Harris said he should judge there must have been twenty people, following him, in all; and one woman with a baby, who had been there all the morning, insisted on taking his arm, for fear of losing him.

Harris kept on turning to the right, but it seemed a long way, and his cousin said he supposed it was a very big maze.

Harris began to think it rather strange himself, but he held on until, at last, they passed the half of a penny bun on the ground that Harris's cousin swore he had noticed there seven minutes ago. Harris said: "Oh, impossible!" but the woman with the baby said, "Not at all," as she herself had taken it from the child, and thrown it down there, just before she met Harris. That made Harris mad, and he produced his map, and explained his theory.

"The map may be all right enough," said one of the party, "if you know whereabouts in it we are now."

Harris didn't know, and suggested that the best thing to do would be to go back to the entrance, and begin again. For the beginning again part of it there was not much enthusiasm; but with regard to the advisability of going back to the entrance there

Maze of Hampton court

was complete unanimity, and so they turned, and trailed after Harris again, in the opposite direction. About ten minutes more passed, and then they found themselves in the centre.

They did know where they were, and the map was once more consulted, and the thing seemed simpler than ever, and off they started for the third time.

And three minutes later they were back in the centre again.

After that, they simply couldn't get anywhere else. Whatever way they turned brought them back to the middle. .

They all got crazy at last, and sang out for the keeper, and the man came and climbed up the ladder outside, and shouted out directions to them. But all their heads were, by this time, in such a confused whirl that they were incapable of grasping anything, and so the man told them to stop where they were, and he would come to them. They huddled together, and waited; and he climbed down, and came in.

Harris said he thought it was a very fine maze, so far as he was a judge; and we agreed that we would try to get George to go into it, on our way back.

Chapter VII

It was while passing through Moulsey Lock that Harris told me about his maze experience. It took us some time to pass through, as we were the only boat, and it is a big lock. I don't think I ever remember to have seen Moulsey Lock, before, with only one boat in it. It is, I suppose, Boulter's not even excepted, the busiest lock on the river.

On a fine Sunday it presents this appearance nearly all day long, while, up the stream, and down the stream, lie, waiting their turn, outside the gates, long lines of still more boats; and boats are drawing near and passing away, so that the sunny river, from the Palace up to Hampton Church, is dotted and decked with yellow, and blue, and orange, and white, and red, and pink. All the inhabitants of Hampton and Moulsey dress themselves up in boating costume, and come and mouch round the lock with their dogs, and flirt, and smoke, and watch the boats.

The boat nears Hampton Church. Harris wanted to get out at Hampton Church, to go and see Mrs. Thomas's tomb.

"Who is Mrs. Thomas?" I asked.

"How should I know?" replied Harris. "She's a lady that's got a funny tomb, and I want to see it."

I objected. I don't know whether it is that I am built wrong, but I never did seem to hanker after tombstones myself. I know that the proper thing to do, when you get to a village or town, is to rush off to the churchyard, and enjoy the graves; but it is a recreation that I always deny myself. I take no interest in creeping round dim and chilly churches behind wheezy old men, and reading epitaphs. Not even the sight of a bit of cracked brass let into a stone affords me what I call real happiness.

One golden morning of a sunny day, I leant against the low stone wall that guarded a little village church, and I smoked, and drank in deep, calm gladness from the sweet, restful scene.

It was a lovely landscape. It was idyllic, poetical, and it inspired me. I felt good and noble. I felt I didn't want to be sinful and wicked any more. I would come and live here, and never do any more wrong, and lead a blameless, beautiful life, and have silver hair when I got old, and all that sort of thing.

In that moment I forgave all my friends and relations for their wickedness and cussedness, and I blessed them. They did not know that I blessed them. They went their abandoned way all

The boat nears Hampton Church

unconscious of what I, far away in that peaceful village, was doing for them. But I did it, and I wished that I could let them know that I had done it, because I wanted to make them happy. I was going on thinking away all these grand, tender thoughts, when my dream was broken in upon by a sharp piping voice crying out:

"All right, sir, I'm a-coming, I'm a-coming. It's all right, sir; don't you be in a hurry."

I looked up, and saw an old bald-headed man hobbling across the churchyard towards me, carrying a huge bunch of keys in his hand that shook and jingled at every step.

I motioned him away with silent dignity, but he still advanced, screeching out the while:

"I'm a-coming, sir, I'm a-coming. I'm a little lame. I ain't as spry as I used to be. This way, sir."

"Go away, you miserable old man," I said.

"I've come as soon as I could, sir," he replied. "My missis never see you till just this minute. You follow me, sir."

"Go away," I repeated; "leave me before I get over the wall, and slay you."

He seemed surprised.

"Don't you want to see the tombs?" he said.

"No," I answered, "I don't. I want to stop here, leaning up against this gritty old wall. Go away, and don't disturb me. I am chock full of beautiful and noble thoughts, and I want to stop like it, because it feels nice and good. Don't you come fooling about, making me mad, chivying away all my better feelings with this silly tombstone nonsense of yours. Go away, and get somebody to bury you cheap, and I'll pay half the expense."

He was bewildered for a moment. He rubbed his eyes, and looked hard at me. I seemed human enough on the outside: he couldn't make it out.

He said:

"You are a stranger in these parts? You don't live here?"

"No," I said, "I don't. *You* wouldn't if *I* did."

"Well then," he said, "you want to see the tombs—graves—folks been buried, you know—coffins!"

"You are an untruther," I replied, getting roused; "I do not want to see tombs—not your tombs. Why should I? We have graves of our own, our family has. Why my uncle Podger has a tomb in Kensal Green Cemetery that is the pride of all that country-side. My grandfather's vault at Bow is capable of accommodating eight visitors, while my great-aunt Susan has a brick grave in Finchley Churchyard. When I want graves, it is to those places that I go and revel. I do not want other folk's. When you yourself are buried, I will come and see yours. That is all I can do for you."

He burst into tears. He said that one of the tombs had a bit of stone upon the top of it that had been said by some to be probably part of the remains of the figure of a man, and that another had some words, carved upon it, that nobody had ever been able to interpret.

I still remained stubborn, and, in broken-hearted tones, he said:

"Well, won't you come and see the memorial window?"

I would not even see that, so he fired his last shot. He drew near, and whispered hoarsely:

"I've got a couple of skulls down in the crypt," he said; "come and see those. Oh, do come and see the skulls! You are a young man out for a holiday, and you want to enjoy yourself. Come and see the skulls!"

Then I turned and fled, and as I sped I heard him calling to me:

"Oh, come and see the skulls; come back and see the skulls!"

Old man approaching J

Harris, however, revels in tombs, and graves, and epitaphs, and monumental inscriptions, and the thought of not seeing Mrs. Thomas's grave made him crazy. He said he had looked forward to seeing Mrs. Thomas's grave from the first moment that the trip was proposed—said he wouldn't have joined if it hadn't been for the idea of seeing Mrs. Thomas's tomb.

I reminded him of George, and how we had to get the boat up to Shepperton by five o'clock to meet him, and then he went for George. Why was George to fool about all day, and leave us to lug this lumbering old top-heavy barge up and down the river by ourselves to meet him? Why couldn't George come and do some work? Why couldn't he have got the day off, and come down with us? Bank be blowed! What good was he at the bank?

"I never see him doing any work there," continued Harris, "whenever I go in. He sits behind a bit of glass all day, trying to look as if he was doing something. What's the good of a man behind a bit of glass? I have to work for my living. Why can't he work. What use is he there, and what's the good of their banks? They take your money, and then, when you draw a cheque, they send it back smeared all over with 'No effects,' 'Refer to drawer.' What's the good of that? That's the sort of trick they served me twice last week. I'm not going to stand it much longer. I shall withdraw my account. If he was here, we could go and see that tomb. I don't believe he's at the bank at all. He's larking about somewhere, that's what he's doing, leaving us to do all the work. I'm going to get out, and have a drink."

I pointed out to him that we were miles away from a pub.; and then he went on about the river, and what was the good of the river, and was everyone who came on the river to die of thirst?

It is always best to let Harris have his head when he gets like this. Then he pumps himself out, and is quiet afterwards.

He said he must drink something, however, and climbed upon the seat, and leant over to get the bottle. It was right at the bottom of the hamper, and seemed difficult to find, and he had to lean over further and further, and, in trying to steer at the same time, from a topsy-turvy point of view, he pulled the wrong line, and sent the boat into the bank, and the shock upset him, and he dived down right into the hamper, and stood there on his head, holding on to the sides of the boat like grim death, his legs sticking up into the air. He dared not move for fear of going over, and had to stay there till I could get hold of his legs, and haul him back, and that made him madder than ever.

Chapter VIII

We stopped under the willows by Kempton Park, and lunched. It is a pretty little spot there: a pleasant grass plateau, running along by the water's edge, and overhung by willows. We had just commenced the third course—the bread and jam—when a gentleman in shirt-sleeves and a short pipe came along, and wanted to know if we knew that we were trespassing. We said we hadn't given the matter sufficient consideration as yet to enable us to arrive at a definite conclusion on that point, but that, if he assured us on his word as a gentleman that we *were* trespassing, we would, without further hesitation, believe it.

He gave us the required assurance, and we thanked him, but he still hung about, and seemed to be dissatisfied, so we asked him if there was anything further that we could do for him; and Harris, who is of a chummy disposition, offered him a bit of bread and jam.

I fancy he must have belonged to some society sworn to abstain from bread and jam; for he declined it quite gruffly, as if he were vexed at being tempted with it, and he added that it was his duty to turn us off.

George with a banjo

Harris said that if it was a duty it ought to be done, and asked the man what was his idea with regard to the best means for accomplishing it. Harris is what you would call a well-made man of about number one size, and looks hard and bony, and the man measured him up and down, and said he would go and consult his master, and then come back and chuck us both into the river.

Of course, we never saw him any more, and, of course, all he really wanted was a shilling. There are a certain number of riverside roughs who make quite an income, during the summer, by slouching about the banks and blackmailing weak-minded noodles in this way. They represent themselves as sent by the proprietor.

We reached Sunbury Lock at half-past three. The river is sweetly pretty just there before you come to the gates, and the backwater is charming; but don't attempt to row up it.

I tried to do so once. I was sculling, and asked the fellows who were steering if they thought it could be done, and they said, oh, yes, they thought so, if I pulled hard. We were just under the little foot-bridge that crosses it between the two weirs, when they said this, and I bent down over the sculls, and set myself up, and pulled.

I pulled splendidly. I got well into a steady rhythmical swing. At the end of five minutes, I thought we ought to be pretty near the weir, and I looked up. We were under the bridge, in exactly the same spot that we were when I began, and there were those two idiots, injuring themselves by violent laughing. I had been grinding away like mad to keep that boat stuck still under that bridge. I let other people pull up backwaters against strong streams now.

We sculled up to Walton, a rather large place for a riverside town. As with all riverside places, only the tiniest corner of it comes down to the water, so that from the boat you might fancy it was a village of some half-dozen houses, all told. Windsor and Abingdon are the only towns between London and Oxford that you can really see anything of from the stream. All the others hide round corners, and merely peep at the river down one street: my thanks to them for being so considerate, and leaving the river-banks to woods and fields and water-works.

At Weybridge, the Wey (a pretty little stream, navigable for small boats up to Guildford, and one which I have always been making up my mind to explore, and never have), the Bourne, and the Basingstoke Canal all enter the Thames together. The lock is just opposite the town, and the first thing that we saw, when we came in view of it, was George's blazer on one of the lock gates, closer inspection showing that George was inside it.

Montmorency set up a furious barking, I shrieked, Harris roared; George waved his hat, and yelled back. The lock-keeper rushed out with a drag, under the impression that somebody had fallen into the lock, and appeared annoyed at finding that no one had.

George had rather a curious oilskin-covered parcel in his hand. It was round and flat at one end, with a long straight handle sticking out of it.

"What's that?" said Harris—"a frying-pan?"

"No," said George, with a strange, wild look glittering in his eyes; "they are all the rage this season; everybody has got them up the river. It's a banjo."

"I never knew you played the banjo!" cried Harris and I, in one breath.

"Not exactly," replied George: "but it's very easy, they tell me; and I've got the instruction book!"

Chapter IX

We made George work, now we had got him. He did not want to work, of course; that goes without saying. He had had a hard time in the City, so he explained. Harris, who is callous in his nature, and not prone to pity, said:

"Ah! and now you are going to have a hard time on the river for a change; change is good for everyone. Out you get!"

He could not in conscience—not even George's conscience—object, though he did suggest that, perhaps, it would be better for him to stop in the boat, and get tea ready, while Harris and I towed, because getting tea was such a worrying work, and Harris and I looked tired. The only reply we made to this, however, was to pass him over the tow-line, and he took it, and stepped out.

Chapter X

George had towed us up to Staines, and we had taken the boat from there, and it seemed that we were dragging fifty tons after us, and were walking forty miles. It was half-past seven when we were through, and we all got in, and sculled up close to the left bank, looking out for a spot to haul up in.

We had originally intended to go on to Magna Charta Island, a sweetly pretty part of the river, where it winds through a soft, green valley, and to camp in one of the many picturesque inlets to be found round that tiny shore. But, somehow, we did not feel that we yearned for the picturesque nearly so much now as we had earlier in the day. A bit of water between a coal-barge and a gas-works would have quite satisfied us for that night. We did not want scenery. We wanted to have our supper and go to bed. However, we did pull up to the point—"Picnic Point," it is called—and dropped into a very pleasant nook under a great elm-tree, to the spreading roots of which we fastened the boat.

Then we thought we were going to have supper, but George said no; that we had better get

Tying the boat to the roots of a tree at picnic point

the canvas up first, before it got quite dark, and while we could see what we were doing. Then, he said, all our work would be done, and we could sit down to eat with an easy mind.

It took us half an hour's hard labour, after that, before it was properly up, and then we cleared the decks, and got out supper.

How good one feels when one is full—how satisfied with ourselves and with the world! People who have tried it, tell me that a clear conscience makes you very happy and contented; but a full stomach does the business quite as well, and is cheaper, and more easily obtained. One feels so forgiving and generous after a substantial and well-digested meal—so noble-minded, so kindly-hearted.

We are but the veriest, sorriest slaves of our stomach. Before our supper, Harris and George and I were quarrelsome and snappy and ill-tempered; after our supper, we sat and beamed on one another, and we beamed upon the dog, too. We loved each other, we loved everybody. Harris, in moving about, trod on George's corn. Had this happened before supper, George would have expressed wishes and desires concerning Harris's fate in this world and the next that would have made a thoughtful man shudder.

And George said: "Not at all;" that it We lit our pipes, and sat, looking out on the quiet night, and talked.

George said why could not we be always like this—away from the world, with its sin and temptation, leading sober, peaceful lives, and doing good. I said it was the sort of thing I had often longed for myself; and we discussed the possibility of our going away, we four, to some handy, well-fitted desert island, and living there in the woods.

We turned in at ten that night, and I thought I should sleep well, being tired; but I didn't. As a rule, I undress and put my head on the pillow, and then somebody bangs at the door, and says it is half-past eight: but, to-night, everything seemed against me; the novelty of it all, the hardness of the boat, the cramped position (I was lying with my feet under one seat, and my head on another), the sound of the lapping water round the boat, and the wind among the branches, kept me restless and disturbed.

Chapter XI

I woke at six the next morning; and found George awake too. We both turned round, and tried to go to sleep again, but we could not.

George tells J. a story about how he once forgot to wind his watch before going to bed. This created confusion and he woke at three in the morning. He realized his mistake when he arrived at work, and aroused the doubt of several constables as he walked around London so late at night.

We had been sitting huddled up in our rugs while George had been telling me this true story, and on his finishing it I set to work to wake up Harris with a scull. The third prod did it: and he turned over on the other side, and said he would be down in a minute, and that he would have his lace-up boots. We soon let him know where he was, however, by the aid of the hitcher, and he sat up suddenly, sending Montmorency, who had been sleeping the sleep of the just right on the middle of his chest, sprawling across the boat.

Then we pulled up the canvas, and all four of us poked our heads out over the off-side, and looked down at the water and shivered. The idea, overnight, had been that we should get up early

George telling a story to J

in the morning, fling off our rugs and shawls, and, throwing back the canvas, spring into the river with a joyous shout, and revel in a long delicious swim. Somehow, now the morning had come, the notion seemed less tempting. The water looked damp and chilly: the wind felt cold.

It was bitterly cold. The wind cut like a knife. I thought I would not throw the water over myself after all. I would go back into the boat and dress; and I turned to do so; and, as I turned, the silly branch gave way, and I and the towel went in together with a tremendous splash, and I was out mid-stream with a gallon of Thames water inside me before I knew what had happened.

"By Jove! old J.'s gone in," I heard Harris say, as I came blowing to the surface. "I didn't think he'd have the pluck to do it. Did you?"

"Is it all right?" sung out George.

"Lovely," I spluttered back. "You are duffers not to come in. I wouldn't have missed this for worlds. Why won't you try it? It only wants a little determination."

But I could not persuade them.

Rather an amusing thing happened while dressing that morning. I was very cold when I got back into the boat, and, in my hurry to get my shirt on, I accidentally jerked it into the water.

It made me awfully wild, especially as George burst out laughing. I could not see anything to laugh at, and I told George so, and he only laughed the more. I never saw a man laugh so much. I quite lost my temper with him at last, and I pointed out to him what a drivelling maniac of an imbecile idiot he was; but he only roared the louder. And then, just as I was landing the shirt, I noticed that it was not my shirt at all, but George's, which I had mistaken for mine; whereupon the humour of the thing struck me for the first time, and I began to laugh. And the more I looked from George's wet shirt to George, roaring with laughter, the more I was amused, and I laughed so much that I had to let the shirt fall back into the water again.

"Ar'n't you—you—going to get it out?" said George, between his shrieks.

I could not answer him at all for a while, I was laughing so, but, at last, between my peals I managed to jerk out:

"It isn't my shirt—it's *yours!*"

I never saw a man's face change from lively to severe so suddenly in all my life before.

"What!" he yelled, springing up. "You silly cuckoo! Why can't you be more careful what you're doing? Why the deuce don't you go and dress on

J accidentally throws the shirt into the water

the bank? You're not fit to be in a boat, you're not. Gimme the hitcher."

I tried to make him see the fun of the thing, but he could not. George is very dense at seeing a joke sometimes.

Harris proposed that we should have scrambled eggs for breakfast. He said he would cook them. The sun had got more powerful by the time we had finished breakfast, and the wind had dropped, and it was as lovely a morning as one could desire.

Slowly the heavy, bright-decked barges leave the shore of Runningmede. Slowly against the swift current they work their ponderous way, till, with a low grumble, they grate against the bank of the little island that from this day will bear the name of Magna Charta Island. And King John has stepped upon the shore, and we wait in breathless silence till a great shout cleaves the air, and the great cornerstone in England's temple of liberty has, now we know, been firmly laid.

Chapter XII

We went over to Magna Charta Island, and had a look at the stone which stands in the cottage there and on which the great Charter is said to have been signed. Though, as to whether it really was signed there, or, as some say, on the other bank at "Runningmede," I decline to commit myself. There are the ruins of an old priory in the grounds of Ankerwyke House, which is close to Picnic Point, and it was round about the grounds of this old priory that Henry VIII. is said to have waited for and met Anne Boleyn. He also used to meet her at Hever Castle in Kent, and also somewhere near St. Albans. It must have been difficult for the people of England in those days to have found a spot where these thoughtless young folk were *not* spooning.

From Picnic Point to Old Windsor Lock is a delightful bit of the river. A shady road, dotted here and there with dainty little cottages, runs by the bank up to the "Bells of Ouseley," a picturesque inn, as most up-river inns are, and a place where a very good glass of ale may be drunk—so Harris says; and on a matter of this kind you can take Harris's word. Old Windsor is a famous spot in its way. Edward the Confessor had a palace here, and

Magna Charta Island

here the great Earl Godwin was proved guilty by the justice of that age of having encompassed the death of the King's brother.

After you pass Old Windsor, the river is somewhat uninteresting, and does not become itself again until you are nearing Boveney. We tugged steadily on to a little below Monkey Island, where we drew up and lunched.

We went through Maidenhead quickly, and then eased up, and took leisurely that grand reach beyond Boulter's and Cookham locks. Clieveden Woods still wore their dainty dress of spring, and rose up, from the water's edge, in one long harmony of blended shades of fairy green. In its unbroken loveliness this is, perhaps, the sweetest stretch of all the river, and lingeringly we slowly drew our little boat away from its deep peace.

We had the river to ourselves, except that, far in the distance, we could see a fishing-punt, moored in mid-stream, on which three fishermen sat; and we skimmed over the water, and passed the wooded banks, and no one spoke.

I was steering.

As we drew nearer, we could see that the three men fishing seemed old and solemn-looking men. They sat on three chairs in the punt, and watched intently their lines. And the red sunset threw a mystic light upon the waters, and tinged with fire the towering woods, and made a golden glory of the piled-up clouds. It was an hour of deep enchantment, of ecstatic hope and longing. The little sail stood out against the purple sky, the gloaming lay around us, wrapping the world in rainbow shadows; and, behind us, crept the night.

We seemed like knights of some old legend, sailing across some mystic lake into the unknown realm of twilight, unto the great land of the sunset.

We did not go into the realm of twilight; we went slap into that punt, where those three old men were fishing. Harris told them they ought to be grateful for a little excitement, sitting there fishing all day, and he also said that he was shocked and grieved to hear men their age give way to temper so.

But it did not do any good.

George said he would steer, after that. He said a mind like mine ought not to be expected to give itself away in steering boats—better let a mere commonplace human being see after that boat, before we jolly well all got drowned; and he took the lines, and brought us up to Marlow.

And at Marlow we left the boat by the bridge, and went and put up for the night at the "Crown."

Chapter XIII

Marlow is one of the pleasantest river centres I know of. It is a bustling, lively little town; not very picturesque on the whole, it is true, but there are many quaint nooks and corners to be found in it. From Marlow up to Sonning is even fairer yet. Grand old Bisham Abbey, whose stone walls have rung to the shouts of the Knights Templars, and which, at one time, was the home of Anne of Cleves and at another of Queen Elizabeth, is passed on the right bank just half a mile above Marlow Bridge. Bisham Abbey is rich in melodramatic properties. It contains a tapestry bed-chamber, and a secret room hid high up in the thick walls. The ghost of the Lady Holy, who beat her little boy to death, still walks there at night, trying to wash its ghostly hands clean in a ghostly basin.

Warwick, the king-maker, rests there, careless now about such trivial things as earthly kings and earthly kingdoms; and Salisbury, who did good service at Poitiers.

Just before you come to the abbey, and right on the river's bank, is Bisham Church, and, perhaps, if any tombs are worth inspecting, they are the

Tombs and monuments of Bisham Church

tombs and monuments in Bisham Church. The famous Medmenham monks, or "Hell Fire Club," as they were commonly called, and of whom the notorious Wilkes was a member, were a fraternity whose motto was "Do as you please," and that invitation still stands over the ruined doorway of the abbey.

Our departure from Marlow I regard as one of our greatest successes. It was dignified and impressive, without being ostentatious.

We had insisted at all the shops we had been to that the things should be sent with us then and there.

We found ourselves short of water at Hambledon Lock; so we took our jar and went up to the lock-keeper's house to beg for some.

George was our spokesman. He put on a winning smile, and said:

"Oh, please could you spare us a little water?"

"Certainly," replied the old gentleman; "take as much as you want, and leave the rest."

"Thank you so much," murmured George, looking about him.

"Where—where do you keep it?"

"It's always in the same place my boy," was the stolid reply: "just behind you."

"I don't see it," said George, turning round.

"Why, bless us, where's your eyes?" was the man's comment, as he twisted George round and pointed up and down the stream.

"There's enough of it to see, ain't there?"

"Oh!" exclaimed George, grasping the idea; "but we can't drink the river, you know!"

"No; but you can drink *some* of it," replied the old fellow. "It's what *I've* drunk for the last fifteen years."

George told him that his appearance, after the course, did not seem a sufficiently good advertisement for the brand; and that he would prefer it out of a pump.

We got some from a cottage a little higher up. I daresay *that* was only river water, if we had known. But we did not know, so it was all right. What the eye does not see, the stomach does not get upset over.

Half-way up the backwater, we got out and lunched; and it was during this lunch that George and I received rather a trying shock.

Harris received a shock, too; but I do not think Harris's shock could have been anything like so bad as the shock that George and I had over the business.

You see, it was in this way: we were sitting in a meadow, about ten yards from the water's edge, and we had just settled down comfortably to feed.

Harris had the beefsteak pie between his knees, and was carving it, and George and I were waiting with our plates ready.

The hamper was close behind us, and George and I both turned round to reach one out.

We were not five seconds getting it. When we looked round again, Harris and the pie were gone!

It was a wide, open field. There was not a tree or a bit of hedge for hundreds of yards.

He could not have tumbled into the river, because we were on the water side of him, and he would have had to climb over us to do it.

George and I gazed all about. Then we gazed at each other.

"Has he been snatched up to heaven?" I queried.

"They'd hardly have taken the pie too," said George.

There seemed weight in this objection, and we discarded the heavenly theory.

"I suppose the truth of the matter is," suggested George, descending to the

Harris's head sticking bolt upright among the tall grass

commonplace and practicable, "that there has been an earthquake."

And then he added, with a touch of sadness in his voice: "I wish he hadn't been carving that pie."

With a sigh, we turned our eyes once more towards the spot where Harris and the pie had last been seen on earth; and there, as our blood froze in our veins and our hair stood up on end, we saw Harris's head—and nothing but his head—sticking bolt upright among the tall grass, the face very red, and bearing upon it an expression of great indignation!

George was the first to recover.

"Speak!" he cried, "and tell us whether you are alive or dead—and where is the rest of you?"

"Oh, don't be a stupid ass!" said Harris's head. "I believe you did it on purpose."

"Did what?" exclaimed George and I.

"Why, put me to sit here—darn silly trick! Here, catch hold of the pie."

And out of the middle of the earth, as it seemed to us, rose the pie—very much mixed up and damaged; and, after it, scrambled Harris—tumbled, grubby, and wet.

He had been sitting, without knowing it, on the very verge of a small gully, the long grass hiding it from view; and in leaning a little back he had shot over, pie and all.

He said he had never felt so surprised in all his life, as when he first felt himself going, without being able to conjecture in the slightest what had happened. He thought at first that the end of the world had come.

Harris believes to this day that George and I planned it all beforehand. Thus does unjust suspicion follow even the most blameless for, as the poet says, "Who shall escape calumny?"

Who, indeed!

Chapter XIV

We caught a breeze, after lunch, which took us gently up past Wargrave and Shiplake. Mellowed in the drowsy sunlight of a summer's afternoon, Wargrave, nestling where the river bends, makes a sweet old picture as you pass it, and one that lingers long upon the retina of memory.

Shiplake is a pretty village, but it cannot be seen from the river, being upon the hill.

The river up to Sonning winds in and out through many islands, and is very placid, hushed, and lonely.

We got out at Sonning, and went for a walk round the village. It is the most fairy-like little nook on the whole river.

It is more like a stage village than one built of bricks and mortar.

Every house is smothered in roses, and now, in early June, they were bursting forth in clouds of dainty splendour.

We roamed about sweet Sonning for an hour or so, and then, it being too late to push on past Reading, we decided to go back to one

The river up to Sonning winds in and out through many islands

of the Shiplake islands, and put up there for the night.

We woke late the next morning, and, at Harris's earnest desire, partook of a plain breakfast, with "non dainties."

Then we cleaned up, and put everything straight (a continual labour, which was beginning to afford me a pretty clear insight into a question that had often posed me—namely, how a woman with the work of only one house on her hands manages to pass away her time), and, at about ten, set out on what we had determined should be a good day's journey.

Chapter XV

We came in sight of Reading about eleven. The river is dirty and dismal here. One does not linger in the neighbourhood of Reading. The town itself is a famous old place, dating from the dim days of King Ethelred, when the Danes anchored their warships in the Kennet, and started from Reading to ravage all the land of Wessex; and here Ethelred and his brother Alfred fought and defeated them, Ethelred doing the praying and Alfred the fighting.

In later years, Reading seems to have been regarded as a handy place to run down to, when matters were becoming unpleasant in London. Parliament generally rushed off to Reading whenever there was a plague on at Westminster; and, in 1625, the Law followed suit, and all the courts were held at Reading. It must have been worth while having a mere ordinary plague now and then in London to get rid of both the lawyers and the Parliament.

Henry I lies buried at Reading, in the Benedictine abbey founded by him there, the ruins of which may still be seen; and, in this same abbey, great John of Gaunt was married to the Lady Blanche.

At Reading lock we came up with a steam launch, belonging to some friends of mine, and they towed us up to within about a mile of Streatley. It is very delightful being towed up by a launch. I prefer it myself to rowing. The run would have been more delightful still, if it had not been for a lot of wretched small boats that were continually getting in the way of our launch, and, to avoid running down which, we had to be continually easing and stopping. It is really most annoying, the manner in which these rowing boats get in the way of one's launch up the river; something ought to done to stop it.

The river becomes very lovely from a little above Reading. The railway rather spoils it near Tilehurst, but from Mapledurham up to Streatley it is glorious. A little above Mapledurham lock you pass Hardwick House, where Charles I played bowls. The neighbourhood of Pangbourne, where the quaint little Swan Inn stands, must be as familiar to the *habitues* of the Art Exhibitions as it is to its own inhabitants.

My friends' launch cast us loose just below the grotto, and then Harris wanted to make out that it was my turn to pull. This seemed to me most unreasonable. It had been arranged in the morning that I should bring the boat up to three miles above Reading. Well, here we were, ten

They look at the floating dead body of a woman

miles above Reading! Surely it was now their turn again.

I could not get either George or Harris to see the matter in its proper light, however; so, to save argument, I took the sculls. I had not been pulling for more than a minute or so, when George noticed something black floating on the water, and we drew up to it. George leant over, as we neared it, and laid hold of it. And then he drew back with a cry, and a blanched face.

It was the dead body of a woman. It lay very lightly on the water, and the face was sweet and calm. It was not a beautiful face. It was too prematurely aged-looking, too thin and drawn, to be that; but it was a gentle, lovable face, in spite of its stamp of pinch and poverty, and upon it was that look of restful peace that comes to the faces of the sick sometimes when at last the pain has left them.

Fortunately for us—we having no desire to be kept hanging about coroners' courts—some men on the bank had seen the body too, and now took charge of it from us.

We found out the woman's story afterwards. Of course it was the old, old vulgar tragedy. She had loved and been deceived—or had deceived herself. Anyhow, she had sinned—some of us do now and then—and her family and friends, naturally shocked and indignant, had closed their doors against her.

Left to fight the world alone, with the millstone of her shame around her neck, she had sunk ever lower and lower. For a while she had kept both herself and the child on the twelve shillings a week that twelve hours' drudgery a day procured her, paying six shillings out of it for the child, and keeping her own body and soul together on the remainder.

Six shillings a week does not keep body and soul together very unitedly. They want to get away from each other when there is only such a very slight bond as that between them; and one day, I suppose, the pain and the dull monotony of it all had stood before her eyes plainer than usual, and the mocking spectre had frightened her. She had made one last appeal to friends, but, against the chill wall of their respectability, the voice of the erring outcast fell unheeded; and then she had gone to see her child—had held it in her arms and kissed it, in a weary, dull sort of way, and without betraying any particular emotion of any kind, and had left it, after putting into its hand a penny box of chocolate she had bought it, and afterwards, with her last few shillings, had taken a ticket and come down to Goring.

It seemed that the bitterest thoughts of her life must have centred about the wooded reaches and the bright green meadows around Goring; but women strangely hug the knife that stabs them, and, perhaps, amidst the gall, there may have mingled also sunny memories of sweetest hours, spent upon those shadowed deeps over which the great trees bend their branches down so low.

She had wandered about the woods by the river's brink all day, and then, when evening fell and the grey twilight spread its dusky robe upon the waters, she stretched her arms out to the silent river that had known her sorrow and her joy. And the old river had taken her into its gentle arms, and had laid her weary head upon its bosom, and had hushed away the pain.

Thus had she sinned in all things—sinned in living and in dying. God help her! and all other sinners, if any more there be.

Goring on the left bank and Streatley on the right are both or either charming places to stay at for a few days. The reaches down to Pangbourne woo one for a sunny sail or for a moonlight row, and the country round about is full of beauty. We had intended to push on to Wallingford that day, but the sweet smiling face of the river here lured us to linger for a while; and so we left our boat at the bridge,

She had wandered about the woods by the river's brink all day

and went up into Streatley, and lunched at the "Bull," much to Montmorency's satisfaction.

They say that the hills on each ride of the stream here once joined and formed a barrier across what is now the Thames, and that then the river ended there above Goring in one vast lake. I am not in a position either to contradict or affirm this statement. I simply offer it.

It is an ancient place, Streatley, dating back, like most river-side towns and villages, to British and Saxon times. Goring is not nearly so pretty a little spot to stop at as Streatley, if you have your choice; but it is passing fair enough in its way, and is nearer the railway in case you want to slip off without paying your hotel bill.

Chapter XVI

We stayed two days at Streatley, and got our clothes washed. We had tried washing them ourselves, in the river, under George's superintendence, and it had been a failure. Indeed, it had been more than a failure, because we were worse off after we had washed our clothes than we were before. Before we had washed them, they had been very, very dirty, it is true; but they were just wearable. *After* we had washed them—well, the river between Reading and Henley was much cleaner, after we had washed our clothes in it, than it was before.

All the dirt contained in the river between Reading and Henley, we collected, during that wash, and worked it into our clothes.

The washerwoman at Streatley said she felt she owed it to herself to charge us just three times the usual prices for that wash. She said it had not been like washing, it had been more in the nature of excavating.

We paid the bill without a murmur.

The neighbourhood of Streatley and Goring is a great fishing centre. There is some excellent fishing to be had here. The river abounds in pike, roach, dace, gudgeon, and eels, just here; and you can sit and fish for them all day.

Some people do. They never catch them. I never knew anybody catch anything, up the Thames, except minnows and dead cats, but that has nothing to do, of course, with fishing! The local fisherman's guide doesn't say a word about catching anything. All it says is the place is "a good station for fishing;" and, from what I have seen of the district, I am quite prepared to bear out this statement.

George and I—I don't know what had become of Harris; he had gone out and had a shave, early in the afternoon, and had then come back and spent full forty minutes in pipeclaying his shoes, we had not seen him since—George and I, therefore, and the dog, left to ourselves, went for a walk to Wallingford on the second evening, and, coming home, we called in at a little river-side inn, for a rest, and other things.

We went into the parlour and sat down. There was an old fellow there, smoking a long clay pipe, and we naturally began chatting. He told us that it had been a fine day to-day, and we told him that it had been a fine day yesterday, and then we all told each other that we thought it would be a fine day to-morrow; and George said the crops seemed to be coming up nicely.

Washing the clothes

After that it came out, somehow or other, that we were strangers in the neighbourhood, and that we were going away the next morning.

Then a pause ensued in the conversation, during which our eyes wandered round the room. They finally rested upon a dusty old glass-case, fixed very high up above the chimney-piece, and containing a trout. It rather fascinated me, that trout; it was such a monstrous fish. In fact, at first glance, I thought it was a cod.

"Ah!" said the old gentleman, following the direction of my gaze, "fine fellow that, ain't he?"

"Quite uncommon," I murmured; and George asked the old man how much he thought it weighed.

"Eighteen pounds six ounces," said our friend, rising and taking down his coat. "Yes," he continued, "it wur sixteen year ago, come the third o' next month, that I landed him. I caught him just below the bridge with a minnow. They told me he wur in the river, and I said I'd have him, and so I did. You don't see many fish that size about here now, I'm thinking. Good-night, gentlemen, good-night."

And out he went, and left us alone.

We could not take our eyes off the fish after that. It really was a remarkably fine fish. We were still looking at it, when the local carrier, who had just stopped at the inn, came to the door of the room with a pot of beer in his hand, and he also looked at the fish.

"Good-sized trout, that," said George, turning round to him.

"Ah! you may well say that, sir," replied the man; and then, after a pull at his beer, he added, "Maybe you wasn't here, sir, when that fish was caught?"

"No," we told him. We were strangers in the neighbourhood.

"Ah!" said the carrier, "then, of course, how should you? It was nearly five years ago that I caught that trout."

"Oh! was it you who caught it, then?" said I.

"Yes, sir," replied the genial old fellow. "I caught him just below the lock—leastways, what was the lock then—one Friday afternoon; and the remarkable thing about it is that I caught him with a fly. I'd gone out pike fishing, bless you, never thinking of a trout, and when I saw that whopper on the end of my line, blest if it didn't quite take me aback. Well, you see, he weighed twenty-six pound. Good-night, gentlemen, good-night."

Five minutes afterwards, a third man came in, and described how *he* had caught it early one morning, with bleak; and then he left, and a stolid, solemn-looking, middle-aged individual came in, and sat down over by the window.

None of us spoke for a while; but, at length, George turned to the new comer, and said:

"I beg your pardon, I hope you will forgive the liberty that we—perfect strangers in the neighbourhood—are taking, but my friend here and myself would be so much obliged if you would tell us how you caught that trout up there."

"Why, who told you I caught that trout!" was the surprised query.

We said that nobody had told us so, but somehow or other we felt instinctively that it was he who had done it.

"Well, it's a most remarkable thing—most remarkable," answered the stolid stranger, laughing; "because, as a matter of fact, you are quite right. I did catch it. But fancy your guessing it like that. Dear me, it's really a most remarkable thing."

And then he went on, and told us how it had taken him half an hour to land it, and how it had broken his rod. He said he had weighed it carefully when he reached home, and it had turned the scale at thirty-four pounds.

The real story of the fish

He went in his turn, and when he was gone, the landlord came in to us. We told him the various histories we had heard about his trout, and he was immensely amused, and we all laughed very heartily.

And then he told us the real history of the fish. It seemed that he had caught it himself, years ago, when he was quite a lad; not by any art or skill, but by that unaccountable luck that appears to always wait upon a boy when he plays the wag from school, and goes out fishing on a sunny afternoon, with a bit of string tied on to the end of a tree.

He said that bringing home that trout had saved him from a whacking, and that even his schoolmaster had said it was worth the rule-of-three and practice put together.

He was called out of the room at this point, and George and I again turned our gaze upon the fish.

It really was a most astonishing trout. The more we looked at it, the more we marvelled at it.

It excited George so much that he climbed up on the back of a chair to get a better view of it.

And then the chair slipped, and George clutched wildly at the trout-case to save himself, and down it came with a crash, George and the chair on top of it.

"You haven't injured the fish, have you?" I cried in alarm, rushing up.

"I hope not," said George, rising cautiously and looking about.

But he had. That trout lay shattered into a thousand fragments—I say a thousand, but they may have only been nine hundred. I did not count them.

We thought it strange and unaccountable that a stuffed trout should break up into little pieces like that.

And so it would have been strange and unaccountable, if it had been a stuffed trout, but it was not.

That trout was plaster-of-Paris.

Chapter XVII

We left Streatley early the next morning, and pulled up to Culham, and slept under the canvas, in the backwater there.

The river is not extraordinarily interesting between Streatley and Wallingford. From Cleve you get a stretch of six and a half miles without a lock. I believe this is the longest uninterrupted stretch anywhere above Teddington, and the Oxford Club make use of it for their trial eights.

But however satisfactory this absence of locks may be to rowing-men, it is to be regretted by the mere pleasure-seeker.

For myself, I am fond of locks. They pleasantly break the monotony of the pull. I like sitting in the boat and slowly rising out of the cool depths up into new reaches and fresh views; or sinking down, as it were, out of the world, and then waiting, while the gloomy gates creak, and the narrow strip of day-light between them widens till the fair smiling river lies full before you, and you push your little boat out from its brief prison on to the welcoming waters once again.

They are picturesque little spots, these locks. The stout old lock-keeper, or his cheerful-looking

They meet other boats and river gossip is exchanged

wife, or bright-eyed daughter, are pleasant folk to have a passing chat with. You meet other boats there, and river gossip is exchanged. The Thames would not be the fairyland it is without its flower-decked locks.

Talking of locks reminds me of an accident George and I very nearly had one summer's morning at Hampton Court.

It was a glorious day, and the lock was crowded; and, as is a common practice up the river, a speculative photographer was taking a picture of us all as we lay upon the rising waters.

I did not catch what was going on at first, and was, therefore, extremely surprised at noticing George hurriedly smooth out his trousers, ruffle up his hair, and stick his cap on in a rakish manner at the back of his head, and then, assuming an expression of mingled affability and sadness, sit down in a graceful attitude, and try to hide his feet.

So I faced round quickly, and took up a position in the prow, where I leant with careless grace upon the hitcher, in an attitude suggestive of agility and strength. I arranged my hair with a curl over the forehead, and threw an air of tender wistfulness into my expression, mingled with a touch of cynicism, which I am told suits me.

As we stood, waiting for the eventful moment, I heard someone behind call out:

"Hi! look at your nose."

I could not turn round to see what was the matter, and whose nose it was that was to be looked at. I stole a side-glance at George's nose! It was all right—at all events, there was nothing wrong with it that could be altered. I squinted down at my own, and that seemed all that could be expected also.

"Look at your nose, you stupid ass!" came the same voice again, louder.

And then another voice cried:

"Push your nose out, can't you, you—you two with the dog!"

Neither George nor I dared to turn round. The man's hand was on the cap, and the picture might be taken any moment. Was it us they were calling to? What was the matter with our noses? Why were they to be pushed out!

But now the whole lock started yelling, and a stentorian voice from the back shouted:

"Look at your boat, sir; you in the red and black caps. It's your two corpses that will get taken in that photo, if you ain't quick."

We looked then, and saw that the nose of our boat had got fixed under the woodwork of the lock, while the in-coming water was rising all around it, and tilting it up. In another moment we should be over. Quick as thought, we each seized an oar, and a vigorous blow against the side of the lock with the butt-ends released the boat, and sent us sprawling on our backs.

We did not come out well in that photograph, George and I. Of course, as was to be expected, our luck ordained it, that the man should set his wretched machine in motion at the precise moment that we were both lying on our backs with a wild expression of "Where am I? and what is it?" on our faces, and our four feet waving madly in the air.

Wallingford, six miles above Streatley, is a very ancient town, and has been an active centre for the making of English history. It was a rude, mud-built town in the time of the Britons, who squatted there, until the Roman legions evicted them; and replaced their clay-baked walls by mighty fortifications, the trace of which Time has not yet succeeded in sweeping away, so well those old-world masons knew how to build.

But Time, though he halted at Roman walls, soon crumbled Romans to dust; and on the ground, in later years, fought savage Saxons and huge Danes, until the Normans came.

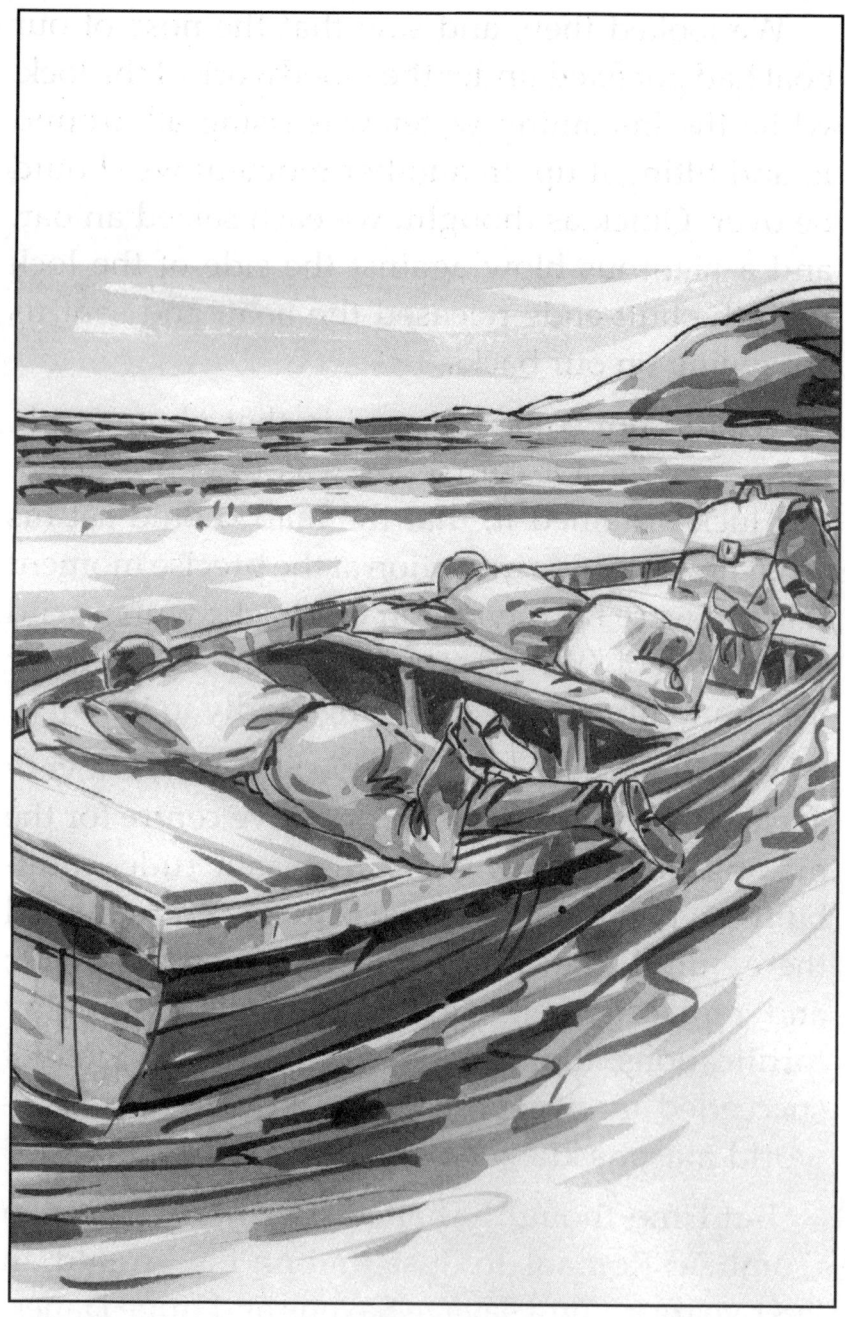

Photo of George and J

It was a walled and fortified town up to the time of the Parliamentary War, when it suffered a long and bitter siege from Fairfax. It fell at last, and then the walls were razed.

From Wallingford up to Dorchester the neighbourhood of the river grows more hilly, varied, and picturesque. Dorchester stands half a mile from the river. It can be reached by paddling up the Thame, if you have a small boat; but the best way is to leave the river at Day's Lock, and take a walk across the fields. Dorchester is a delightfully peaceful old place, nestling in stillness and silence and drowsiness.

Dorchester, like Wallingford, was a city in ancient British times; it was then called Caer Doren, "the city on the water." In more recent times the Romans formed a great camp here, the fortifications surrounding which now seem like low, even hills. In Saxon days it was the capital of Wessex. It is very old, and it was very strong and great once. Now it sits aside from the stirring world, and nods and dreams.

Round Clifton Hampden, itself a wonderfully pretty village, old-fashioned, peaceful, and dainty with flowers, the river scenery is rich and beautiful. If you stay the night on land at Clifton, you cannot do better than put up at the "Barley Mow." It is, without exception, I should say, the quaintest, most old-world inn up the river. It stands on the right of the bridge, quite away from the village. Its low-pitched gables and thatched roof and latticed windows give it quite a story-book appearance, while inside it is even still more once-upon-a-timeyfied.

We were up early the next morning, as we wanted to be in Oxford by the afternoon. It is surprising how early one *can* get up, when camping out. One does not yearn for "just another five minutes" nearly so much, lying wrapped up in a rug on the boards of a boat, with a Gladstone bag for a pillow, as one does in a featherbed. We had finished breakfast, and were through Clifton Lock by half-past eight.

From Clifton to Culham the river banks are flat, monotonous, and uninteresting, but, after you get through Culhalm Lock—the coldest and deepest lock on the river—the landscape improves.

At Abingdon, the river passes by the streets. Abingdon is a typical country town of the smaller order—quiet, eminently respectable, clean, and desperately dull. It prides itself on being old, but whether it can compare in this respect with Wallingford and Dorchester seems doubtful. A famous abbey stood here once, and within what is left of its sanctified walls they brew bitter ale nowadays.

In St. Nicholas Church, at Abingdon, there is a monument to John Blackwall and his wife Jane, who both, after leading a happy married life, died on the very same day, August 21, 1625; and in St. Helen's Church, it is recorded that W. Lee, who died in 1637, "had in his lifetime issue from his loins two hundred lacking but three." If you work this out you will find that Mr. W. Lee's family numbered one hundred and ninety-seven. Mr. W. Lee—five times Mayor of Abingdon—was, no doubt, a benefactor to his generation, but I hope there are not many of his kind about in this overcrowded nineteenth century.

From Abingdon to Nuneham Courteney is a lovely stretch. Nuneham Park is well worth a visit. It can be viewed on Tuesdays and Thursdays. The house contains a fine collection of pictures and curiosities, and the grounds are very beautiful.

The pool under Sandford lasher, just behind the lock, is a very good place to drown yourself in. The undercurrent is terribly strong, and if you once get down into it you are all right. An obelisk marks the spot where two men have already been drowned, while bathing there; and the steps of the obelisk are generally used as a diving-board by young men now who wish to see if the place really *is* dangerous.

Between Iffley and Oxford is the most difficult bit of the river

We passed through Iffley Lock at about half-past twelve, and then, having tidied up the boat and made all ready for landing, we set to work on our last mile.

Between Iffley and Oxford is the most difficult bit of the river I know.

First the current drives you on to the right bank, and then on to the left, then it takes you out into the middle, turns you round three times, and carries you up stream again, and always ends by trying to smash you up against a college barge.

Of course, as a consequence of this, we got in the way of a good many other boats, during the mile, and they in ours, and, of course, as a consequence of that, a good deal of bad language occurred.

Chapter XVIII

We spent two very pleasant days at Oxford. There are plenty of dogs in the town of Oxford. Montmorency had eleven fights on the first day, and fourteen on the second, and evidently thought he had got to heaven.

Among folk too constitutionally weak, or too constitutionally lazy, whichever it may be, to relish up-stream work, it is a common practice to get a boat at Oxford, and row down. For the energetic, however, the up-stream journey is certainly to be preferred. It does not seem good to be always going with the current. There is more satisfaction in squaring one's back, and fighting against it, and winning one's way forward in spite of it—at least, so I feel, when Harris and George are sculling and I am steering.

To those who do contemplate making Oxford their starting-place, I would say, take your own boat—unless, of course, you can take someone else's without any possible danger of being found out. The boats that, as a rule, are let for hire on the Thames above Marlow, are very good boats. They are fairly water-tight; and so long as they are handled with care, they rarely come to pieces,

A boy with the damaged boat

or sink. There are places in them to sit down on, and they are complete with all the necessary arrangements—or nearly all—to enable you to row them and steer them.

But they are not ornamental. The boat you hire up the river above Marlow is not the sort of boat in which you can flash about and give yourself airs. The hired up-river boat very soon puts a stop to any nonsense of that sort on the part of its occupants. That is its chief—one may say, its only recommendation.

The man in the hired up-river boat is modest and retiring. He likes to keep on the shady side, underneath the trees, and to do most of his travelling early in the morning or late at night, when there are not many people about on the river to look at him.

When the man in the hired up-river boat sees anyone he knows, he gets out on to the bank, and hides behind a tree.

I was one of a party who hired an up-river boat one summer, for a few days' trip. We had none of us ever seen the hired up-river boat before; and we did not know what it was when we did see it.

We had written for a boat—a double sculling skiff; and when we went down with our bags to the yard, and gave our names, the man said:

"Oh, yes; you're the party that wrote for a double sculling skiff. It's all right. Jim, fetch round *The Pride of the Thames*."

The boy went, and re-appeared five minutes afterwards, struggling with an antediluvian chunk of wood, that looked as though it had been recently dug out of somewhere, and dug out carelessly, so as to have been unnecessarily damaged in the process.

My own idea, on first catching sight of the object, was that it was a Roman relic of some sort,—relic of *what* I do not know, possibly of a coffin.

The neighbourhood of the upper Thames is rich in Roman relics, and my surmise seemed to me a very probable one; but our serious young man, who is a bit of a geologist, pooh-poohed my Roman relic theory, and said it was clear to the meanest intellect (in which category he seemed to be grieved that he could not conscientiously include mine) that the thing the boy had found was the fossil of a whale; and he pointed out to us various evidences proving that it must have belonged to the preglacial period.

To settle the dispute, we appealed to the boy. We told him not to be afraid, but to speak the plain truth: Was it the fossil of a pre-Adamite whale, or was it an early Roman coffin?

Joining the boat with strings

The boy said it was *The Pride of the Thames*.

We thought this a very humorous answer on the part of the boy at first, and somebody gave him twopence as a reward for his ready wit; but when he persisted in keeping up the joke, as we thought, too long, we got vexed with him.

"Come, come, my lad!" said our captain sharply, "don't let us have any nonsense. You take your mother's washing-tub home again, and bring us a boat."

The boat-builder himself came up then, and assured us, on his word, as a practical man, that the thing really was a boat—was, in fact, *the* boat, the "double sculling skiff" selected to take us on our trip down the river.

We grumbled a good deal. We thought he might, at least, have had it whitewashed or tarred—had *something* done to it to distinguish it from a bit of a wreck; but he could not see any fault in it.

He even seemed offended at our remarks. He said he had picked us out the best boat in all his stock, and he thought we might have been more grateful.

We fastened the so-called boat together with some pieces of string, got a bit of wall-paper and pasted over the shabbier places, said our prayers, and stepped on board.

They charged us thirty-five shillings for the loan of the remnant for six days; and we could have bought the thing out-and-out for four-and-sixpence at any sale of drift-wood round the coast.

The weather changed on the third day,—Oh! I am talking about our present trip now,—and we started from Oxford upon our homeward journey in the midst of a steady drizzle.

The river—with the sunlight flashing from its dancing wavelets, gilding gold the grey-green beech-trunks, glinting through the dark, cool wood paths, chasing shadows o'er the shallows, flinging diamonds from the mill-wheels, throwing kisses to the lilies, wantoning with the weirs' white waters, silvering moss-grown walls and bridges, brightening every tiny townlet, making sweet each lane and meadow, lying tangled in the rushes, peeping, laughing, from each inlet, gleaming gay on many a far sail, making soft the air with glory— is a golden fairy stream.

But the river—chill and weary, with the ceaseless rain-drops falling on its brown and sluggish waters, with a sound as of a woman, weeping low in some dark chamber; while the woods, all dark and silent, shrouded in their mists of vapour, stand like ghosts upon the margin; silent ghosts with eyes reproachful,

Rowing the boat all day

like the ghosts of evil actions, like the ghosts of friends neglected—is a spirit-haunted water through the land of vain regrets.

We rowed on all that day through the rain, and very melancholy work it was. We pretended, at first, that we enjoyed it. We said it was a change, and that we liked to see the river under all its different aspects. We said we could not expect to have it all sunshine, nor should we wish it. We told each other that Nature was beautiful, even in her tears.

Indeed, Harris and I were quite enthusiastic about the business, for the first few hours. And we sang a song about a gipsy's life, and how delightful a gipsy's existence was!—free to storm and sunshine, and to every wind that blew!—and how he enjoyed the rain, and what a lot of good it did him; and how he laughed at people who didn't like it.

George took the fun more soberly, and stuck to the umbrella.

We hoisted the cover before we had lunch, and kept it up all the afternoon, just leaving a little space in the bow, from which one of us could paddle and keep a look-out. In this way we made nine miles, and pulled up for the night a little below Day's Lock.

I cannot honestly say that we had a merry evening. The rain poured down with quiet persistency. Everything in the boat was damp and clammy. Supper was not a success. Cold veal pie, when you don't feel hungry, is apt to cloy. I felt I wanted whitebait and a cutlet; Harris babbled of soles and white-sauce, and passed the remains of his pie to Montmorency, who declined it, and, apparently insulted by the offer, went and sat over at the other end of the boat by himself.

George requested that we would not talk about these things, at all events until he had finished his cold boiled beef without mustard.

We played penny nap after supper. We played for about an hour and a half, by the end of which time George had won four pence—George always is lucky at cards—and Harris and I had lost exactly two pence each.

We thought we would give up gambling then. As Harris said, it breeds an unhealthy excitement when carried too far. George offered to go on and give us our revenge; but Harris and I decided not to battle any further against Fate.

After that, we mixed ourselves some toddy, and sat round and talked. George told us about a man he had known, who had come up the river two years ago and who had slept out in

Playing cards

a damp boat on just such another night as that was, and it had given him rheumatic fever, and nothing was able to save him, and he had died in great agony ten days afterwards. George said he was quite a young man, and was engaged to be married. He said it was one of the saddest things he had ever known.

And that put Harris in mind of a friend of his, who had been in the Volunteers, and who had slept out under canvas one wet night down at Aldershot, "on just such another night as this," said Harris; and he had woke up in the morning a cripple for life. Harris said he would introduce us both to the man when we got back to town; it would make our hearts bleed to see him.

This naturally led to some pleasant chat about sciatica, fevers, chills, lung diseases, and bronchitis; and Harris said how very awkward it would be if one of us were taken seriously ill in the night, seeing how far away we were from a doctor.

There seemed to be a desire for something frolicksome to follow upon this conversation, and in a weak moment I suggested that George should get out his banjo, and see if he could not give us a comic song.

He at once fished out his instrument, and commenced to play "Two Lovely Black Eyes."

I had always regarded "Two Lovely Black Eyes" as rather a commonplace tune until that evening.

The rich vein of sadness that George extracted from it quite surprised me.

The desire that grew upon Harris and myself, as the mournful strains progressed, was to fall upon each other's necks and weep; but by great effort we kept back the rising tears, and listened to the wild yearnful melody in silence.

The second day was exactly like the first. The rain continued to pour down, and we sat, wrapped up in our mackintoshes, underneath the canvas, and drifted slowly down.

One of us—I forget which one now, but I rather think it was myself—made a few feeble attempts during the course of the morning to work up the old gipsy foolishness about being children of Nature and enjoying the wet; but it did not go down well at all. That—

"I care not for the rain, not I!" was so painfully evident, as expressing the sentiments of each of us, that to sing it seemed unnecessary.

On one point we were all agreed, and that was that, come what might, we would go through with this job to the bitter end.

We had come out for a fortnight's enjoyment on the river, and a fortnight's enjoyment on the river we meant to have.

If it killed us! well, that would be a sad thing for our friends and relations, but it could not be helped. We felt that to give in to the weather in a climate such as ours would be a most disastrous precedent.

"It's only two days more," said Harris, "and we are young and strong. We may get over it all right, after all."

At about four o'clock we began to discuss our arrangements for the evening. We were a little past Goring then, and we decided to paddle on to Pangbourne, and put up there for the night.

"Another jolly evening!" murmured George.

We sat and mused on the prospect. We should be in at Pangbourne by five.

We should finish dinner at, say, half-past six. After that we could walk about the village in the pouring rain until bed-time; or we could sit in a dimly-lit bar-parlour and read the almanac.

"Why, the Alhambra would be almost more lively," said Harris, venturing his head outside the cover for a moment and taking a survey of the sky.

Coming back home

"With a little supper at the — to follow," I added, half unconsciously.

"Yes it's almost a pity we've made up our minds to stick to this boat," answered Harris; and then there was silence for a while.

"If we *hadn't* made up our minds to contract our certain deaths in this bally old coffin," observed George, casting a glance of intense malevolence over the boat, "it might be worth while to mention that there's a train leaves Pangbourne, I know, soon after five, which would just land us in town in comfortable time to get a chop, and then go on to the place you mentioned afterwards."

Nobody spoke. We looked at one another, and each one seemed to see his own mean and guilty thoughts reflected in the faces of the others.

In silence, we dragged out and overhauled the Gladstone. We looked up the river and down the river; not a soul was in sight!

Twenty minutes later, three figures, followed by a shamed-looking dog, might have been seen creeping stealthily from the boat-house at the "Swan" towards the railway station, dressed in the following neither neat nor gaudy costume:

Black leather shoes, dirty; suit of boating flannels, very dirty; brown felt hat, much battered; mackintosh, very wet; umbrella.

We had deceived the boatman at Pangbourne. We had not had the face to tell him that we were running away from the rain.

We had left the boat, and all it contained, in his charge, with instructions that it was to be ready for us at nine the next morning.

If, we said—*if* anything unforeseen should happen, preventing our return, we would write to him.

We reached Paddington at seven, and drove direct to the restaurant I have before described, where we partook of a light meal, left Montmorency, together with suggestions for a supper to be ready at half-past ten, and then continued our way to Leicester Square.

We attracted a good deal of attention at the Alhambra. On our presenting ourselves at the paybox we were gruffly directed to go round to Castle Street, and were informed that we were half-an-hour behind our time.

We convinced the man, with some difficulty, that we were *not* "the world-renowned contortionists from the Himalaya Mountains," and he took our money and let us pass.

Inside we were a still greater success. Our fine bronzed countenances and picturesque clothes were followed round the place with admiring gaze. We were the cynosure of every eye.

It was a proud moment for us all.

We adjourned soon after the first ballet, and wended our way back to the restaurant, where supper was already awaiting us.

I must confess to enjoying that supper. For about ten days we seemed to have been living, more or less, on nothing but cold meat, cake, and bread and jam.

It had been a simple, a nutritious diet; but there had been nothing exciting about it, and the odour of Burgundy, and the smell of French sauces, and the sight of clean napkins and long loaves, knocked as a very welcome visitor at the door of our inner man.

We pegged and quaffed away in silence for a while, until the time came when, instead of sitting bolt upright, and grasping the knife and fork firmly, we leant back in our chairs and worked slowly and carelessly—when we stretched out our legs beneath the table, let our napkins fall, unheeded, to the floor, and found time to more critically examine the smoky ceiling than we had hitherto been able to do—when we rested our glasses at arm's-length upon the table, and felt good, and thoughtful, and forgiving.

Montmorency barks in agreement

Then Harris, who was sitting next the window, drew aside the curtain and looked out upon the street.

It glistened darkly in the wet, the dim lamps flickered with each gust, the rain splashed steadily into the puddles and trickled down the waterspouts into the running gutters. A few soaked wayfarers hurried past, crouching beneath their dripping umbrellas, the women holding up their skirts.

"Well," said Harris, reaching his hand out for his glass, "we have had a pleasant trip, and my hearty thanks for it to old Father Thames—but I think we did well to chuck it when we did. Here's to Three Men well out of a Boat!"

And Montmorency, standing on his hind legs, before the window, peering out into the night, gave a short bark of decided concurrence with the toast.

Post-Reading Activities

1. In what ways are Harris and J.'s Uncle Podger similar?

2. Write about Harris' visit to the maze at Hampton Court.

3. How do the three friends pack for their trip?

4. What was the reason to reject the sea trip?

5. Why was Harris against the idea of camping?

6. Which incident did you find most humorous?

7. Who was Montmorency?